YSOBELLA BLACK

Paranormal
Short & Steamy Stories

OUBLIETTE 2
MERROW

Table of Contents

WORKS BY THE AUTHOR

All of my stories and series, except for Alix in Wonderland and Raven Chronicles, are a different aspect of my Dragaverse, but can be read and enjoyed as standalone.

Stories by Ysobel Black
(Nice/Sweet Versions)

Bakery Street Cozy Mysteries

Paranormal Cozy Mysteries
The Lyrical Lycanthrope

Fairy Tales With a Twist

Retellings of fairy tales, myths, and stories you only thought you knew.
The Crimson Hood & the Alpha of Wolves
The Ice Maiden & the Princes of Diamonds

Holiday Hullabaloo

Love in Ashana can be tricky, but twelve days of chaos result in paranormal happily-ever-afters.
A Penghou in a Pine Tree
Two Tatzelwurms
Three French Bêtes
Four Ceffyl Dŵr
Five Golden Wings

Six Grootslangs Playing
Seven Spawns a-Swimming
Eight Maenads Mixing
Nine Lazy Dragons
Ten Swords a-Sneaking
Eleven Pixie Potions
Twelve Lovers Loving

Pohjola Maidens

The Maidens of Pohjola are free, heading for the human world, and looking for love.
Dream's Sleeper: Lemminki

Strygoi Witches & Vampires

Join an Ildum of vampires over 10,000 years of history and mythology as they find their Dragăs — witches who make their hearts beat and restore their souls.
Ember's Light: Stryx
Viktoria's Shadow: Jael
Myth's Legend: Norrix
Bijou's Cure: Zeke
Musette's Fate: Idris

Strygoi Witches & Vampires Companion Stories

Shadowy — Viktoria's prequel (companion novella)
Echo's Answer: Lachlan (companion novel)

Stories by Ysobella Black
(Naughty/Steamy Versions)

Alix in Wonderland

A reverse harem (MFMMM) retelling of Alice in Wonderland.
Madness of the Hatter

Bakery Street Mysteries

Paranormal Cozy-ish Mysteries
The Lyrical Lycanthrope

Fairy Tales With a Kink

Retellings of fairy tales, myths, and stories you only thought you knew.
The Crimson Hood & the Alpha of Wolves
The Ice Maiden & the Princes of Diamonds

Grove of Bandrui

Immortal Druids search for their Maités.
Druid of Oaks
Druid of Apples

Harom & Aneja

Witches choose three men to form their Haroms as they become Aneja
— Walkers in magic. Reverse Harem (MFMM)
RealmWalker
BeastWalker

Magical Love in London

Regency London with a Paranormal twist
A Marriage of Inconvenience

Oubliette

Paranormal Short and Steamy Stories
Selkie
Merrow

Pohjola Passions

The Maidens of Pohjola are free, heading for the human world, and
looking for love.
Dream's Sleeper: Lemminki

Raven Chronicles: Phoenix Rising

An epic spanning generations — the battle for the Raven Throne is full
of sex, intrigue, and betrayal.
First Generation

Souls Lost & Found

Under a Blue Moon, star-crossed lovers get a second chance for their love to shine.
The Egyptian

Utopia Pack Shifters

A pack of shifters find their Fateds.
Unyielding

Vampires & Strygoi Witches

Join an Ildum of vampires over 10,000 years of history and mythology as they find their Dragăs — witches who make their hearts beat and restore their souls.
Ember's Light: Stryx
Viktoria's Shadow: Jael
Myth's Legend: Norrix
Bijou's Cure: Zeke
Musette's Fate: Idris

Vampires & Strygoi Witches Companion Stories

Shadowy — Viktoria's Prequel (Companion Novella)
Echo's Answer: Lachlan (Companion Novel)

Xuterias: Xov & Xau

Enemies to Lovers Paranormal Romances
Poisoned Heart

<u>Yuletide Chaos</u>

Short Paranormal Romances about finding love in mystical Ashana.
A Penghou in a Pine Tree
Two Tatzelwurms
Three French Bêtes
Four Ceffyl Dŵr
Five Golden Wings
Six Grootslangs Playing
Seven Spawns a-Swimming
Eight Maenads Mixing
Nine Lazy Dragons
Ten Swords a-Sneaking
Eleven Pixie Potions
Twelve Lovers Loving
12 Days of Chaos Box Set

COLLECTIONS/BOX SETS
<u>Three First in a Series</u>
<u>FATED – Three Firsts</u>
Ember's Light:Stryx
RealmWalker
Poisoned Heart

<u>Five First in a Series</u>

<u>FATED – Five Firsts</u>
Ember's Light:Stryx
The Crimson Hood & the Alpha of Wolves
RealmWalker
Dream's Sleeper: Lemminki
Poisoned Heart

<u>Vampires & Strygoi Witches</u>
<u>COLLECTION ONE: BOOKS 1-4</u>

<u>Yuletide Yearnings</u>
DAYS 1-12

https://ysobellablack.com/newsletter[1]

---

1. https://ysobellablack.com/newsletter/

CHAPTER ONE

STEPHANIE

STEPHANIE SHOULDERED her way into the foyer, only half listening to Tessa through the earpiece. Her best friend had fallen in love recently — as in two days ago — and was doing her best to spread love like a contagion.

"— birthday tomorrow. You can't spend it alone."

The idea of spending it as third wheel didn't appeal, either. Stephanie climbed the staircase to the second floor of her home. "I was going to have dinner with Mom and Dad, but they left yesterday because my sister is having my latest nephew. Maybe I'll go to the beach." She dumped her books on the desk and flopped onto her bed.

Tessa's laughter echoed through the speaker. "*You*? Go into *nature*?"

"I know! It's crazy, but for the last week, I've had the strangest urge to go into the ocean, even though that place is full of things that sting, bite, and could swallow me whole, and I'd never even see it coming. Nature is psycho."

"Well, we should do something for your birthday. Let me think and I'll call you back."

"All right. Say hi to your new man and I'll talk to you later."

Disconnecting the call, Stephanie removed her earpiece and lay back. Now what? Dinner and a movie? A book? No.

A reward.

She'd aced her Humanities test, hadn't she? Only one final left for the semester, and that wasn't until next week. She deserved to celebrate, and her favorite way to do that nowadays was a trip to Oubliette.

Stephanie sat up and examined her reflection in the closet door mirror. Just a touchup to her eyeliner and a dash of lipstick needed. Fortunately, she'd not unleashed her wild auburn hair yet. Wrestling that hot mess back into sleekness would take ages.

Yes. She deserved a trip to Oubliette.

The downtown bar was more than the dive it appeared to be. The club under the dive bar facade catered to fantasies — entry required a mask and a safeword.

A vision of sun-kissed skin, muscled abs, bulging biceps, and thick thighs filled her mind. Triton's turquoise eyes and silvery hair fascinated her. His coloring was unusual, but suited him.

Of course, she couldn't be sure Triton was his actual name, and had never seen his full face — just a strong jawline, the flash of white teeth in the dark, sharp cheekbones. The rest of his face always remained hidden behind a turquoise-blue half mask with gold trim that matched hers.

Drive or take the tunnels? The city had been a pirate and smuggler haven at one time, and was riddled with secret passages and underground tunnels. The secret passage from her house joined a network under the city.

Going by car would be faster, but traveling by the secret passages always made her trips to Oubliette even more illicit. Even if spiders insisted on building their webs everywhere.

Decided, she opened her closet and pulled her mask from the shelf. Halfway down a staircase leading to the basement, she stopped and pressed a knothole on a riser. A wooden panel on the wall clicked open.

Stephanie picked up one of the flashlights stored there, shut the panel, and followed the tunnel until it joined the main network leading into the city.

Following the tunnels had become habit, and she tracked her turns by memory. There were hundreds of offshoots. A few had collapsed over time, and others, like the one leading to her house, had been blocked with locked doors. Most were open and went from downtown all the way to the lighthouse.

The passage ended in what resembled a never-used sewer. It had been blocked forever, but mysteriously cleared a month ago. She climbed a ladder on the concrete wall, and opened the door into an alley.

Oubliette was behind a nondescript metal door that opened into a typical dive bar. Lighting was dim. The air smelled of beer. Requisite pool tables and dart boards stood opposite a long wooden bar lined with stools. A few tables and booths filled the space in between. Bottles of alcohol lined shelves behind the bar.

None of that interested her tonight.

She entered what she thought of as the Hall of Masks — decorated in red and black and lit only by a candle-filled chandelier that sent shadows dancing over the masks hanging on the walls. The selection of masks was different every time she visited, but none of the new ones ever appealed to her.

"Good evening." The receptionist sat behind a sleek, black desk. The only things to hand were a little black book, and an old-fashioned rotary telephone. She always wore an elaborately decorated gown and a full-face mask with feathers and glitter. "What can Oubliette do for... or to, you today?"

Stephanie had met the woman a few times, but she'd never offered her name. She wore a different mask every time, but her voice was the same, and she always seemed to be here, no matter the time or day.

"Hello. Is Triton here tonight?"

The masked woman consulted her little black book. "He is. One moment." Lifting the handset of her telephone, she murmured a few words, and hung up. "He'll be waiting for you. Safeword?"

"Sushi."

"Welcome."

A thrill went through Stephanie as the trap door opened and she went down a steep winding staircase that exited onto a hallway full of closed doors. She never saw or heard anyone else in the communal areas, but Triton had taken her to a few places where she could peer through windows into private rooms, bringing out a naughty voyeur side of herself she hadn't thought existed.

Stephanie unlocked her assigned room and went in. Lingerie and costumes hung on a rack. Toys and restraints filled rows of shelves. Whatever she wanted to use, she'd take in with her.

What did she want to play with today? She dressed in a lacy bra, barely there panties, garters, stockings, a silk nightie, and thigh-high boots with six inch heels. Her Triton did so love to tear clothes off her. Well, she liked it when he ripped her clothes off, too, like he couldn't control himself because she drove him crazy.

She'd felt an instant connection to her mystery man the moment they'd met. Loved turning herself over to him and letting him push her boundaries. He always knew just what she needed, and she liked to think, given how he reacted to her, that he felt the same way.

When she entered the room, Triton was already there. Six-and-a-half feet of dominating man leaned against the wall. His long silver hair was braided and draped over one shoulder, and he wore only leather pants.

The decor was different this time. A cross, benches, one sofa, and the four-poster bed were gone, making way for a much larger canopy bed.

And dark velvet curtains were closed over a window.

A window.

The idea of being the watched rather than the watcher did something fluttery to her stomach.

Triton ran his eyes over her in a look so scorching she felt it on her skin. When he reached her eyes again, he winked. "Did you wear those boots so you're taller than me, baby?"

Yes, but she wouldn't admit to it. She lifted her chin. The stiletto heels gave her about half an inch on him.

He backed her against the wall. "Enjoy it while it lasts. I'm going to have you on your back and your knees. Your boots won't help you then." He slid a finger over her thigh, around the top of one boot.

"I'm going to destroy your pretty little lace outfit. I think we'll leave the boots on, though."

True to his word, he swept her into his arms and tossed her on the bed. It took him all of two seconds to get her on her back.

"Have you waited for me, Stephanie?"

She nodded, and he trailed his finger over her belly to her mound.

He paused. "I can tell if you're lying. Your pussy will be swollen and weeping for me if you haven't been satisfied. Now, let me see."

Stephanie slid her fingers under the elastic of her thong and wiggled to push it to her knees. She lifted her legs, parted her thighs, and leaned back on her elbows.

Lying in this position, completely exposed to him, while he stared at her core was unnerving, and she found herself wanting to squirm or break the silence.

An appreciative grin pulled at the corners of his mouth, and she relaxed.

He strolled over, moving like a sleek jungle cat who owned the world. When he reached her, he trailed a finger over the tip of her breast. The nipple hardened, begging for attention, and her breath caught.

Triton moved between her legs and crawled up the bed. She raised her hips. His hand touched her inner thigh, then went to where she needed him. "You're soaking wet. Have you been thinking of what I'm going to do to you?"

"Yes," she whispered. One touch to her clit, one finger inside her would set her off.

He parted her and traced the lines of her inner lips, then took one of her hands, rubbing her finger where his were.

"Feel how swollen you are? Your slick is seeping out of your pussy and pooling here." He lowered his finger against the pucker of her ass, and she jumped.

He used her finger to caress her tight hole for another moment before releasing it. She moved to touch her clit, desperate to orgasm, but he stopped her. She'd waited long enough! Stephanie growled in frustration, pulling against his hold.

"Oh, no, baby, this is mine. You've waited this long. You don't want to go even longer without being fucked, do you?"

"No!"

Triton ripped the panties off her, but left her thigh-high boots on, placing one on spiked heel against each of his shoulders. When he leaned forward, her legs spread wider.

His silvery head lowered toward her pussy, and his mouth fell on her hot center. Sucking her throbbing clit into his mouth, he slid a finger into her. He slipped his hand under her ass and lifted her.

"Triton!" She panted when he dipped his tongue inside her. Her fingers entangled in his hair, drawing him closer as her head fell back and she rode his face.

He ran his tongue over her clit while sliding another finger into her, then spread her further to slip three fingers inside her.

Stephanie tugged on his hair and cried out as she came in a heated rush. The muscles of her sheath gripped his fingers before he slid them away from her. He licked, sucked, and tongued her to two more orgasms.

He was never stingy with her pleasure, making her come often and so easily. The things he did with his tongue were probably illegal in some states. When he let her come up for air, she sagged, relaxed and sated.

"Get on your knees and face the window. Put your hands above your head and cross them at the wrists."

She glanced between him and the closed curtain and moved into position. Would people be watching? Had they already seen Triton make her orgasm? Would she be able to watch the audience watching her?

Triton bound her wrists to an overhead support for the canopy, slightly behind her. Her chest pushed out, on display because of her slightly arched position.

He stood and unbuttoned his pants, sliding his zipper down. His huge cock jutted out, moisture glistening at the tip. His hand encircled his girth and pumped.

Triton moved onto the bed behind her and tangled a hand in her hair to pull her head back. "I'm going to blindfold you and open the curtain. You won't know if anyone is watching you or not."

An anticipatory shiver ran through her.

Emerald silk slid over her skin giving her the chance to refuse. She didnt. He covered her eyes over her mask.

She heard his pants hit the floor, the bed dipped behind her, and his hands were on her, tilting her hips. He coated his cock in her slickness, aligned himself with her opening, and pushed into her with one thrust.

"Triton!" She moaned as he slid home and pulled out, then thrust along her sex. The head of his dick rubbed her clit.

Leaning past her, he slid the curtain open, the rings sliding along the rod.

Her only focus was the movement of his cock, gliding against her clit with every stroke.

He caressed the cheeks of her ass, making her squirm before pushing the huge head of his cock against the slick lips of her pussy. She wiggled her hips, trying to entice him inside. Instead, he glided through her slickness, before slipping back against her ass. Was he going to take her there in front of everyone?

"Time for you to work, baby. Take it deep, and ride me." His dick pressed at her entrance and she lowered herself on his massive width until he was deep inside. His big body tensed, but he waited for her to set the pace. Her body arched further as her hips circled and bucked.

"Feels so good." They groaned together as she leaned forward as much as she could, letting him take her weight and allowing him deeper.

He used his hold on her hips to slam her up and down on his length. The shudder that ran through her was exhilaration. Was someone watching them? Getting off on her getting off?

She moaned, falling headlong into her release.

Before she could brace herself, he slammed into her pussy, shoving her body up and rattling the chains. Something pushed against her puckered hole.

"Triton?" Stephanie tried to look over her shoulder at him even though she couldn't see him.

His hand stroked her back. "Shhh, don't think, baby, just feel." His hand slipped from her back and around to her clit. As he tweaked the bundle of nerves, he pushed his finger into her ass.

She clenched against his sudden intrusion. "Triton!" Her breasts bounced wildly as he set a relentless pace.

"Give me your mouth, baby."

Stephanie turned her head. His tongue licked at her lips in teasing caresses, forcing her to seek more.

She tried to take in the sensations. Triton invaded every part of her. The twinge of discomfort only amplified the feel of his cock buried inside her.

With her hands bound, unable to brace or see, she was completely at his mercy.

CHAPTER TWO

TRITON

TRITON NEVER FELT SO powerful as when he fucked his mate. He shuddered and pulled his cock out before slamming back in. He moved his tongue in her mouth, and the finger in her ass in tempo with his thrusts into her pussy, increasing the pace. His dick swelled impossibly large, setting off a wave of contractions inside her.

The tight, wet muscles of her sheath clenching him were nearly his undoing as her hips rose and fell.

He tore her nightie off. He had to slow down or this would be over too quickly.

Triton stilled his hips and put his hands on hers to guide her, taking control and forcing her to move in long, slow motions, hitting the places they both needed stroked.

His fangs extended when he slid his hands over her breasts and bent his head to kiss her neck. He had no restraint over them right now, something that only happened with her. He always kept them carefully sheathed when he was with sex partners, but there was no keeping anything leashed with Stephanie.

She writhed and fought to speed up their pace. His torture was abated by the knowledge she was equally as tormented. Within moments, she clenched around him, seeking more contact — that little bit more that would send her into orgasm.

Her lacy scrap of a bra went next, tossed over his shoulder. He pulled her against him, pressing his arm across her breasts, so she was stripped but not bared to any onlookers. His other hand covered her mound as he toyed with her clit.

He powered forward again, driving into her body vigorously. A body made for sin. A body made for him. Her head fell back, and pants escaped her as her back arched.

"Please!" she begged. That was his undoing. He drove into her with a frenzy bordering on insanity, and found himself doing the one thing he'd never been tempted to do before. His needle-like fangs sank into Stephanie's shoulder, and he clamped down.

The serum transfering from him to her, given on a consistent basis, would change her body, making it easier to be his mate, and eventually bear his offspring. Taking his semen inside her would change her, too.

Triton expected her to scream or thrash when he pierced her flesh. Instead, she became more wild as she met each one of his thrusts. He kept her pinned in place against him as he went into full rut. He licked at the bite, tasting her blood. He released her hip to rub her clit, needing to feel her come one more time.

The muscles of her sheath constricted so forcefully around him that she wrenched his seed from him. Her body convulsed around his length. His hips rose as he slammed into her one, two, three more times before stiffening with his release.

Throwing his head back, he bellowed in possession as he came into her in a stream that seemed to go on endlessly. His body was wracked by the new sensations of this deeper, more potent release. He didn't care if everyone in Oubliette heard. They would all know she was his.

His mate.

Her climaxing muscles continued to grasp him within her delectable body, milking more seed from him until she sagged in her chains.

"Fuck, baby!" He leaned against her back, his cock still twitching inside her.

Holding her close against him, he inhaled the scent of him all over her, mingled with sex and blood. When their breathing calmed, he reached up and released the blindfold and bindings, catching her weight as her arms dropped. He closed the curtain and curled himself around her.

As he rubbed her shoulders to ease her muscles, something protective stirred within him as he gently eased her back and rose to his feet. She watched as he walked across the room, grabbed the pitcher of water and retrieved a towel.

He wet the towel before returning to her and gently cleaning her. Her hands curled into the bed. Tossing the towel aside, he bent to kiss her before crawling into bed with her and pulling her into his arms as her limp, sated body relaxed against him.

TRITON CLIMBED THE stairs to return to the bar. It had filled a bit more since he left. The pool tables were all in use, and thirsty patrons lined up at the bar, where Maclyr and Xinthos poured drinks.

"Hey." Maclyr rattled a shaker and filled several martini glasses. Laugh lines formed around his topaz eyes when he smirked.

Smug Selkie had already figured out how to get his mate.

Who came here for martinis? Where had martini glasses come from? Next thing he knew, there'd be olives, cherries, and paper umbrellas everywhere.

A quick scan of the bar revealed several women at a booth in the back. They wore sashes and tiaras. They must have been the martini drinkers. Oubliette was going to lose its dive bar reputation.

Xinthos, purplish eyes knowing, winked at Triton. As an Incubus, he fed on the energies in the bar — life, magic, and, of course, sex. He slid shot glasses to several customers.

"Hey." Triton shuddered inwardly. The shots were probably the firewater Xinthos brewed. It was always surprising no one actually spontaneously combusted when they drank the concoction. It was made especially for Other Worlders who needed a bit more kick to their drink.

He ducked behind the bar and slipped into effortless coordination with Maclyr and Xinthos.

When they had a break, Maclyr wiped his hands on a towel. "Did you know it's Stephanie's birthday tomorrow?"

Triton frowned. "No." He did know his Stephanie was best friends with Maclyr's mate Tessa. The women had discovered Oubliette together.

"Oh. Well, Tessa wants to do something special for Stephanie. Apparently, she's recently developed an interest in the ocean. Shocking, right?" Maclyr arched one dark eyebrow. "Anyway, I said I would ask you if we could rent a boat for a few hours."

Stephanie's new affinity for the ocean was another sign she was his mate. He'd bitten her tonight. Marked her. If he kept doing it, she would develop telepathic abilities. Her blood would hold more oxygen. She wouldn't become Merrow herself — there was no way to change her body so completely, but any children he sired on her would be full Merrow.

Participants weren't supposed to see visitors to Oubliette outside the club. Wards and spells kept them separated outside the play rooms. The chance to see Stephanie away from Oubliette was too much temptation.

Maclyr and Tessa had met at the club. He'd known she was his mate immediately, but it wasn't until they'd met outside the club that they'd made their relationship official.

Triton wasn't going to miss out on the opportunity to do the same with Stephanie. "When do you want to go out?"

"Tomorrow morning? I know it's short notice, but Tessa couldn't plan things like this before."

Because she'd lived as a prisoner of her father until Maclyr stole her away a couple of days ago.

"I'm off tomorrow. We can go out on my boat."

CHAPTER THREE

STEPHANIE

"WE'RE GOING OUT ON *that*?" Stephanie laughed. She'd expected a inflatable zodiac or fishing boat when Tessa had called all excited last night and said to meet them at the yacht club to go for a boat ride. Not this fifty foot yacht. Tessa always did like to do things big.

The gleaming white vessel was huge, at least to her. Rows of portholes and balconies lined the sides, and several levels had different sized outside decks front and back. Kayaks were lashed to one side of a rear deck. Stairs and metal rungs led from level to level.

There were even larger boats in the harbor. How did things so enormous even float? That made no sense.

Several people already moved around the boat. Tessa was easy to spot, along with her new man, Maclyr. Stephanie's phone had blown up with photos of the new couple over the last two days. Two more men, shirtless, one blond, the other dark, both sleekly muscled, moved around on different decks.

Stephanie shifted her beach bag on her shoulder and walked down the maze of wooden docks, flip-flops smacking into her heels.

"Happy birthday, Stephanie." Tessa rushed down a staircase and pushed a box wrapped in shiny green paper into Stephanie's chest as she stepped onto the yacht.

"Thank you." Stephanie hugged Tessa, then pushed her to arm's length. Her friend had a new sparkle to her eyes, a bigger smile, and a lighter step. Could be her new love. Or being free of chains she'd worn her whole life. "Freedom looks good on you, my friend."

Tessa grinned. "Feels good, too." She took Stephanie's hand and pulled her up the stairs. "Come meet our captain. He's on the bridge."

Stephanie's mouth went dry as she caught sight of the captain. Long silver hair loose, the man was shirtless and barefoot, wearing a pair of board shorts as he talked to three other men.

It was her Triton. She'd know that expanse of muscled chest anywhere, even if she didn't feel that strange pull toward him, or recognize that silver hair.

Stephanie gripped Tessa's arm hard enough to bruise. "You didn't say *he* would be here!'

"I didn't?" Tessa smirked. "I'm sure I meant to. This is his boat."

"Tessa!" Stephanie wore ragged clothes, no makeup, and her hair had a mind of its own. In short, she was a mess, and in the bright of day, while he was sexy without even trying! It was hardly fair.

"Triton is friends with Maclyr and offered the use of his boat. He won't care if you're wearing your third best shorts and oldest favorite t-shirt."

"And my second best bikini!" He couldn't know who she was. It was fine. Plenty of women were named Stephanie. That's what wearing the masks alt the club was all about, right?

Tessa snorted. "Any man would appreciate you in any bikini."

"It's just so weird to see him outside of Oubliette." Although she wasn't complaining. She'd seen him naked in the darkness of Oubliette, but watching him move around the yacht in the light of day, he seemed even more predatory in his easy way of ownership.

Triton's turquoise eyes found her mortified face, ran up and down her body in a hot look that felt like a caress, and he winked at her.

Oh, God. He'd given her *that* look before. He knew who she was without her mask, just like she knew who he was.

Suddenly, everything felt real. With that shield ripped away, she felt more naked than she'd ever been with him. Despite that, the larger part of her couldn't help being drawn to him. And she was no wallflower. She could pretend they didn't know each other better naked.

Her feet took the necessary steps and she stopped in front of him. She met his bemused expression with defiance. Annoyed he felt this was funny, she carried the charade to an extreme.

"Hello. I'm Stephanie. I'm told this is your boat. Thank you for allowing us aboard this morning." She extended her hand for a shake. "It's nice to meet you..."

Maclyr choked on his drink and Tessa laughed. Bad friend. Not helpful. The other two men Triton had been talking to glanced between him and her.

That sexy mouth of his curved into a smile. "Triton." He enclosed her hand in his larger one, running his thumb over her inner wrist as he raised her fingers to his lips and kissed them.

Damn the man. The pressure of his lips and quick flick of his tongue on her skin sent hot flutters through her.

The blond grinned at her. "I'm Finn." He jabbed a thumb over his shoulder at the dark-haired man. "He's Sheol."

"If you need *anything*, Stephanie," Triton murmured, "come for me. I am happy to do whatever it takes to give you the most pleasurable experience possible."

"Seriously?" Stephanie whispered furiously. "Come for you?" She tried to take her hand back.

Triton didn't let her. "Of course." He gave her a totally fake, wide-eyed, innocent look. "I'll be on the bridge. So you must come for me if you need anything."

Stephanie narrowed her eyes at him. "I think you mean come *find* you."

"My mistake. English is not my first language." He released her hand and climbed metal rungs to the next deck. "Cast off."

Finn and Sheol didn't hide their smirks as they moved to release the ropes.

WITH THE BREEZE ON her face, Stephanie fixed her eyes on the ocean, wishing she could see beneath the waves. The yacht was nice, but she wanted to be closer — to touch the sea.

She didn't need to see him to know Triton walked up behind her. He put his hands on the rail on either side of her, caging her in the circle of his arms.

"How's the trip? Do you have anywhere in particular you wanted to go? There are a number of islands we can visit."

"It's amazing, but I don't know where to go. I've never been on a boat before."

He lowered his head to her ear and bit her earlobe. "You've not come for me."

"I can't believe you said that in front of everyone!"

He chuckled in her ear, making goosebumps flow over her skin. "Happy Birthday, baby. You should have told me."

"You're not meant to know who I am."

"I will always recognize you. But now I have to improvise a suitable gift, don't I?"

"The boat trip is —"

One hand moved to her thigh, his quick and clever fingers under the edge of her shorts before she realized he'd moved. She caught her breath as he stroked her pussy over the thin material of her bikini bottom. "If you hold perfectly still and don't make a sound, you can come for me right now in front of everyone, and they won't even know."

He knew her too well.

"This isn't Oubliette."

"That's right. Here your kinks don't hide behind a mask. They're all yours."

His light touch did everything to her and nothing for her. She moaned low in her throat as he circled her clit.

"Yes or no, Stephanie?"

Say yes.

She jumped at the unexpected voice in her head, but let the strangeness go as Triton's fingers grew more insistent. She wanted to agree anyway.

"Yes."

Triton shoved the edge of her bikini bottom aside and his thick fingers were on her flesh. He stroked her slit from top to bottom, stopping to apply more pressure to her clit in slow circles. The pace had her restless. Her hips chased his hand, trying to get more pressure where she needed it. She moaned in frustration, until he slipped a finger in her pussy, sinking it in to his palm. Her breath quickened. It wouldn't take much to push her over.

She was tempted to look around. Was anyone watching? Could they hear how wet she was, and the sounds Triton's fingers made inside her?

"No, baby. You stare at the ocean."

His hand moved faster. Pressure built inside her. She felt helpless to do anything but let him touch her. There was nothing she could have said or done to stop him.

"Come for me, Stephanie," he rasped. His finger pressed hard and her world exploded into a pulsing wave of pleasure.

He stroked her through the orgasm and kept touching her. Like he was going to make her come again.

Stephanie reached for her frayed control. "What are you doing?"

"I think you can come again before anyone notices."

She pushed on his wrist, detaching his fingers from her body. Her pussy protested with a slick greedy sound as she took a step sideways. Scambling for anything to divert her attention from the way she still wanted his touch, her eyes landed on the kayaks.

"Can we go out on the kayaks?" Then she'd be closer to the sea. "Please?"

"Have you ever used one before?"

"No."

Triton scanned the sky and sea around them. He nodded. "The sea is calm. I'll go with you." He raised his voice. "Take us to the forest."

Sheol's face popped over the railing right over their heads. "Aye, Captain."

Stephanie jumped. Had he been there the whole time? She cleared her throat as color seeped up her neck. "The forest?"

"The kelp forest. You should be able to see fish, turtles, and at least one seal." Triton busied himself unstowing kayaks. "Anyone else want to go out? There's also snorkeling gear and drysuits in the lockers."

"I'd like to snorkel." Tessa led Maclyr downstairs to Stephanie.

He hugged Tessa from behind. "I'll help you suit up." They entered the locker room.

When the yacht engine idled, Triton lowered two single kayaks into the ocean. "This area is nice. We're over kelp beds. Then we can head for those sea caves." He pointed at some black rocks that sprawled over the surface of the sea.

"Thank you for doing this." Stephanie met his eyes as she kicked off her flip-flops, feeling shy. It was strange being around him as a normal person.

"You're welcome." He held out a hand for her.

The kayak wobbled as she stepped onto the seat. She gripped Triton's hand tight, afraid the kayak would slip from under her feet like a banana peel in the movies.

"It's all right. Sit. You'll feel more balanced."

She bent her knees and slid her legs into the hollow space in front of her.

"Here." Tessa, now dressed in some kind of baggy suit, handed over the green-paper wrapped gift in one gloved hand. "Just in case. You never know when an emergency might happen."

"An emergency? Did you get me an emergency beacon or something?"

Tessa bit her lip, and nodded. "Or something!"

Rolling her eyes, Stephanie tucked the box under the netting on the front of her kayak.

The water was so clear she could see to the bottom of the kelp forest. Golden-orange stalks grew tall, swaying with the gentle swells of the ocean. Their leaves provided cover for fish darting beneath her. Something larger moved — a flash of green shell. A sea turtle!

A sable-colored seal popped his head up in front of her, bumping playfully into her kayak and making her laugh.

Two furry forms holding hands floated by on their backs. Sea otters! They looked cute, but were really little terrors, like gremlins.

Stephanie drew her fingers through the water, feeling a sort of peace run through her.

Why did this feel so natural when she and nature mutually hated each other?

CHAPTER FOUR

TRITON

TRITON DIDN'T LIKE the look of the boat following his yacht. It had only been two days since he'd helped blow up the house of a hunter preying on Other Worlders, and he expected retaliation of some sort from the remaining team members.

His pod of Merrow had helped evacuate the Selkies. A hunter watching them could have tracked the Merrow from the Selkies.

Should they go back to the yacht? Return to the harbor?

He glanced forward to Stephanie, where she paddled enthusiastically, head down as she glided over the kelp beds and peered into them. The boat was hovering there, watching rather than an active threat.

No. Stephanie was enjoying herself, and he was enjoying watching her outside Oubliette.

What would she think if she knew the seal bumping into her kayak was Maclyr? Triton chuckled. It was unlikely Tessa had explained her new man spent time as a seal.

How would Stephanie react when Triton explained about Merrow? He knew her body well, but most of her personality was a mystery.

Monitor the other boat. He directed the thought at the other Merrow aboard the yacht. All of them could communicate telepathically — necessary when speaking wasn't possible underwater.

We see them, Finn replied. *They seem to be more interested in monitoring what we do than attacking.*

A gentle current drifted them toward the seacave. It didn't look like much, but there was a surprise inside. "The entrance is narrow. Just use your paddle to push off the rocks if you scrape the sides."

"Got it. I love kayaking."

Perfect. She'd never swim as well as him, but after he explained about Merrow and mates, she could kayak while he was in his other form.

The cave entrance curved to the left, losing the majority of sunlight.

"I can't see a thing in here."

"Trust me?"

"You know I do."

With her body and sexual pleasure, yes. But this was a different kind of trust. Triton felt like puffing out his chest. He leaned toward Stephanie. His eyes worked well enough in near darkness. They had to at depth in the sea.

"Put your paddle across your lap, and close your eyes until I say to open them." He took hold of her kayak and guided them into a narrow tunnel. It opened into a vast chamber that arced overhead. Hundreds of glowworms covered the ceiling and walls.

"Open your eyes."

She did, and gasped. "They're like little stars!"

"You like stars, Stephanie?" He liked saying her name and seeing her without a mask. She had an expressive face.

"Especially the ones I can wish on." She sounded wistful, and the tone tugged at his heart.

"What do you wish for?" If he could grant it, he would. He had access to all manner of magic and treasures.

"I —"

Something slammed into the cave on the outside, shaking the entire place.

What the fuck?

Triton leapt from his kayak, stripped off his shorts in the water, and shifted to his Merrow form. His legs melded as scales and tattoos grew over his body. The skin between his fingers and toes stretched to form webbing. Able to move faster now, he pushed Stephanie's kayak toward the tunnel as she shrieked.

"Hang on."

Another boom echoed through the seacave. A boulder fell from the ceiling and smashed into the back of the kayak, tearing the front out of his hands. Stephanie screamed as she flew into the air, then went silent as she hit the wall and splashed into the water.

"Stephanie!"

Triton lunged for her. His fingers brushed her still form as another boulder fell, crashing onto his back. Bones snapped inside him, sending half his body numb, then filling with agony. He lost his grip on his mate, sinking below the surface under the weight of the rock.

Pain radiated from his spine to the rest of his body, momentarily stunning him as he sank. His eyes dilated and gills erupted on his neck as he went deeper.

More boulders rained down around him. The entire cave system was falling on his head. And Stephanie was unconscious, incapable of getting out of danger! Were rocks hitting her? Was she facedown and drowning? Could she hold her breath longer with so little of his serum in her blood?

The seabed rushed toward him. A streak of agony went down his left side as he twisted in a desperate attempt to avoid being crushed. He pulled his tail away, narrowly avoiding tearing his fin as the boulder hit the bottom.

Triton pushed off the sand, but something was definitely wrong inside him as he swam awkwardly toward the surface. He found Stephanie face down in the water, flipped her onto her back and listened to her chest.

Her heart beat, but she wasn't breathing.

He sealed his mouth over hers and exhaled into her. She coughed and breathed on her own. Triton ran his hands over her, searching for anything broken or bleeding, and found only a small bump on her head. Relief gusted out of him.

Now to get Stephanie out of here.

The damaged kayak floated nearby, but it wouldn't go far. The back was crushed, the paddle lost. He lifted Stephanie and slid her into the seat, letting her slump forward.

The narrow gap of the entrance was half filled with rubble, but the impacts seemed to be done. Hunters must have assaulted the cave. They might be waiting to see if he came out.

But Stephanie and Tessa were human, not Other Worlders. Did Tessa's father know his hunters considered his daughter acceptable collateral damage?

Triton couldn't risk taking Stephanie out of the cave if enemies awaited. He guided the kayak to a low overhang and wedged it in place. Changing to human, he clambered up the rockslide and peered outside.

A storm raged. Gray thunderclouds whirled in the sky and rain fell in sheets. Flashes of lightning lit the clouds. Waves hit twenty feet high and wind gusted with near hurricane force.

The tempest out of the clear blue sky could only have come from one place — the defensive magic on his yacht.

Sheol? Finn?

Neither answered.

Triton squinted through the downpour. His yacht was gone. They'd only have used the spell if they were under attack.

It made sense they'd left. This storm was no place for a yacht. There were hundreds of islands in the bay where they could find shelter. No sign of the other ship, either. They must have drawn it away.

The Merrow could jump overboard, and Maclyr was a Selkie. Between them, they'd make sure Tessa was safe, even if they had to abandon ship, and she'd already been wearing a drysuit.

Stephanie needed his help more, and in no condition to travel far. The cold would be sapping her body heat now that she'd been soaked in the ocean. There was an island close by he could take her to.

He pushed and shoved rocks out of his way. The lower the blockage, the easier to wrestle the kayak out.

Gunfire erupted, sending chips of stone up around him. A searing sensation tore through his side.

Triton gritted his teeth and whirled. His assailant was almost invisible, perched on the edge of the black rocks and wearing scuba gear, including a helmet that enclosed his head and probably had communications. He carried an underwater rifle in addition to the gun he pointed at Triton. These hunters were well supplied. Not surprising, considering they were funded by Tessa's millionaire father.

This hunter must have been abandoned when his ship left. Or was destroyed. Triton hoped the ship had been taken out of the equation.

He dove below the surface into darkness, changed to Merrow, and immersed himself within the current and surge. Letting his innate sense of the ocean guide him, he lined himself up under the hunter, and arrowed through the water at his attacker. At the crest of the wave, Triton leapt from the water and crashed into the man.

The action cost Triton in pain, but the hunter dropped his weapon. Grappling, the pair of them tumbled down the slope into the crashing waves.

On his home territory, Triton drew strength from the sea, unlike his opponent. For all his weapons and gear, the man fighting him was only human. Underwater, his blows had no power to them.

Glad something was finally going his way, Triton slammed his fist into the hunter's unprotected gut.

They rose to the surface and a wave swept them up. It carried them straight toward the jagged, unforgiving rocks of the sea cave. Triton released his hold on the hunter and used his flagging strength to turn back into the ocean.

The hunter wasn't so fortunate or streamlined. His body crashed into the rocks, flailing arms and legs going still.

Riding the next wave, Triton landed next to the hunter. He'd not survived.

Unable to muster any sympathy, Triton left the hunter's body and sank below the surface to a depth where the sea didn't roil. He let the water roll over him and give him the power he needed for his next job.

Get Stephanie somewhere safe and dry.

The poor kayak took more abuse as its sides and bottom scraped over sharp stones. He shoved the craft through the tunnel, gritting his teeth against his injuries.

Finally through, Triton held the kayak from underneath, guiding it with powerful strokes of his tail. There was an island not far away where they could get out of the current and storm. He wouldn't last much longer.

For the first time, swimming was a chore. Every flick of his tail sapped his remaining strength. Rain colder than the ocean pelted his skin. He put a hand to his side, bringing away bloody fingertips. The bullet wound was healing, but not quickly enough. His back ached, but the stabbing agony of broken bones had subsided.

The island came into sight. A speck of land with a freshwater spring, rudimentary shelter, and a tangle of trees. He lay in the ocean, willing himself to heal faster. The rain stopped. Paused, more accurately. It would start again soon.

Shoving the kayak onto the beach, he shifted to his human form and staggered up the sand. Triton summoned his remaining strength, slipped his arms around Stephanie, and lifted her with a groan.

The small hut wasn't much, but was dry. He dragged his feet through the soft sand and shouldered through the weathered wooden door that never closed properly.

Stephanie shivered in his arms. Triton stripped her wet clothes off, wrung her wild curls as dry as possible, placed her on the bed, and covered her with blankets. He kindled a fire in the stove and hung up her bikini, shorts, and shirt. They'd dry quickly with the warmth of the stove heating the small space.

They didn't keep much here, but he could offer a hot drink and soup when she woke. He dressed in a spare pair of board shorts, picked up a pail, and headed for the spring to get fresh water.

He dipped the bucket into the water, filled it, and set it down. His ass hit the ground next to it. Exhaustion weighed on him. Like he'd only been able to stay in motion because he was already in motion, and now that he'd stopped, he couldn't start again.

His eyelids closed and he struggled to open them.

Five seconds. He could rest for five seconds, then he'd go to his mate.

Hang on, Stephanie.

CHAPTER FIVE

STEPHANIE

HANG ON, STEPHANIE.

What was that voice? She was too young to be losing her mind.

Shut up, voice. I don't want to talk to you.

Thankfully, the voice obeyed.

Stephanie opened her eyes and stared at a ceiling made of crooked, rough-hewn planks. She closed her eyes and opened them again. The strange ceiling was still there.

Her clothes were not. Naked wasn't ideal. She turned her head to examine the rest of her accommodation. Heat came from a stove. Her clothes hung from the low ceiling. A few cabinets hung on the walls, and a rickety dresser stood opposite the bed.

Her head ached, and her lungs burned. She touched the sore place on her skull. Her fingers moved over a small bump, but came away blood free.

Where was she? What happened?

The cave-in.

Triton! He was there with her. Had he brought her here? That was the best scenario, rather than a stranger stripping her while she was unconscious. But where had he gone?

She rolled to her side and pushed herself to sitting. After a moment of lightheadedness, she stood and pulled on her mostly dry clothes.

Stephanie stepped outside. The air smelled like rain and gray clouds filled the sky.

Turning around, she examined the shelter.

A hut. It listed to the side, and looked like a strong breeze would knock it the rest of the way over. The plants and trees weren't exactly a jungle, but the idea of traipsing into the thicket with bare arms and legs, and without shoes, held no appeal.

There might be snakes. Or spiders. Snakes *and* spiders. Scorpions. Bugs carrying deadly diseases. Any number of creepy crawlies that stung or bit could be lying in wait.

Plants were dangerous, too. Pretty leaves could make her skin itch or break out in hideous rashes. Treacherous trees might drop a coconut on her head and kill her, or offer delicious looking fruit that was really poisonous.

Stephanie did *not* do nature.

"Triton?" Waiting a few seconds, she called louder, "Triton?" She did some rough calculations. About three hours on the yacht. Stephanie cupped her hands around her mouth. "Professor? MaryAnn?" They were the sensible ones.

No answer. It was probably better that way. She wasn't sure she was ready to face a stranger, even a TV character. Stephanie sighed and followed a trail that led away from the hut. At least the island was sandy and soft on her bare feet.

Her kayak lay beached high on the sand. The gift from Tessa lay trapped in the netting, looking a bit soggy. Hopefully it wasn't completely ruined.

Unlike the kayak — which was half smashed and had no paddle.

Where was the other kayak? And Triton? If he wasn't here, who had been taking care of her?

"Triton?"

The rain had stopped, but the sea roiled in huge gray waves. No way to get off the island right now, even if she could use the kayak. Turning to the right, she headed down the beach. Maybe someone lived on the island.

Green parrots squawked as they flew overhead, and an orange iguana stared suspiciously at her. "Right back at you, buddy. You just stay over there and we'll be fine."

After a tour of sand, trees, and stinky seaweed full of buzzing flies, she was back where she'd started, with no sign of anyone else in the last hour.

And the freezing rain started again.

Where was Triton? Had be abandoned her? Gone for help in that crazy ocean and drowned? No one knew where she was.

Deflated, Stephanie sank onto the sand under the meager cover of the hut, clutching her birthday present to her chest. She swiped a single tear away. "This better be something useful, Tessa. Like a satellite phone, or a radio. Or an actual emergency beacon."

Stephanie ripped open the soggy green wrapping paper and giggles burst from her chest.

A vibrator.

Well, that wasn't useful in the way she'd hoped in her stranded on a deserted island scenario, but could be useful. She tore the packaging open. Three speeds. Nice thickness.

Batteries not included.

She searched through the packaging again and let out a bellow of frustration.

Are you kidding me, Tessa?

Stephanie was done.

It wasn't bad enough she'd been shipwrecked. Or kayak-wrecked. Whichever. Maybe both. She'd been outed to Triton, and knocked unconscious in a cave-in. Stripped by some mysterious, and apparently invisible, person, who may or may not talk in her head. And now, she was abandoned on a deserted island, surrounded by nature that wanted to kill her. But the biggest injustice of all...

"I'm a woman trapped on an island with a vibrator and no fucking batteries!"

Worst. Birthday. Ever.

CHAPTER SIX

TRITON

A WOMAN'S ANGRY ROAR drilled into Triton's head and snapped his eyes open.

I'm a woman trapped on an island with a vibrator and no fucking batteries!

Triton wheezed a laugh that hurt his ribs. The world had better beware. His mate had a powerful sex drive. Gods help humanity if she didn't get her orgasms.

He touched his bullet wound. Still bleeding, but not as much. Too many injuries too quickly had taxed his healing ability. Climbing to his feet, he picked up the bucket of water, and staggered through the rain toward the hut. He'd slept longer than he'd meant to, yet all he wanted to do was go back to sleep.

Through the open door, Stephanie paced in the hut, as well as she could. It was only large enough to take a few steps in each direction.

"Stephanie." He braced himself on the doorframe.

She halted and whirled for the door. "Triton!" Stephanie threw herself into his arms. He tried not to wince, but failed.

"You're hurt." She took the bucket, slid under his arm, and supported him to a rickety chair, where he sat heavily.

"I'm all right."

"Uh." Her eyes ran up and down his body. "I never thought I'd say this, but you're not looking so hot. You're bleeding. That is *not* all right.

Does that hole go all the way through?" She moved behind him. "It does! Were you stabbed? Your back is one giant bruise!"

"I'll heal."

Stephanie rummaged in the drawers and came up with a clean t-shirt that she wadded up and pressed to his back. "You need stitches. Is there a first aid kit? You've got sand in an open wound. The least we need to do is clean this out."

His mate was adorable when she fretted over him. "Try in the cabinets." Triton leaned back and watched her. She was a dervish as she tore through the hut on a mission to find what she needed. "There's a kettle you can boil water with, plus instant drinks and soup. Help yourself to whatever you find."

"Where were you before? I walked around the island and didn't see you."

"At the spring behind the hut."

Stephanie poured water into the kettle and set it on the stove. She picked up the empty pail. "Where's the spring?"

Triton pointed at the door. "It's pouring. Just set the bucket outside. Rainwater is clean."

"Oh. I've never been trapped on an island before." She set the bucket outside and found the first aid kit. "There's not much in here, but there are some painkillers. Do you want aspirin?"

"No. I just need time to heal."

"You keep saying that." She held up some glue. "What about this? Can we super glue you?"

"Yes." Seemed like Stephanie needed to be useful. The glue wasn't necessary, but it wouldn't hurt. "That'll stop the bleeding. The other option is to cauterize the punctures."

Stephanie's complexion took on a greenish hue. "I'm a big fan of the glue plan. Let's do that." She cleaned out both sides of the bullet wound, applied the glue, and taped bandages onto him, looking pleased with herself.

Trying to hide the true extent of his injuries from her exhausted him more than he expected. When she was finished, he stripped out of his wet shorts, happily collapsed into bed, and half closed his eyes. He fought off sleep as she combed his tangled hair with her fingers.

When the next kettle of water boiled, Stephanie poured it into the soup containers and stirred them. She brought one to the bed and held up a spoonful of vegetable soup.

Was she kidding? "I'm capable of feeding myself."

"Do I need to make choo-choo sounds, or move the spoon around like an airplane? I have young, picky nephews. I *will* get this spoon in your mouth, one way or another."

He glared at her.

"You lost a lot of blood. You need to eat so your body can replace it."

Too tired to argue, he capitulated and opened his mouth. He'd thought it would be humiliating to be fed like an infant, but seeing how Stephanie relaxed as she took care of him blunted his embarrassment enough to finish two meals.

"You've fed me twice. Eat something yourself. I refuse more until you've fed yourself."

Triton could hardly keep his eyes open as she ate and cleaned up. "Enough. You're making me tired just watching you." He held up the bedding to invite her in. "Come to bed and we'll sort everything out in the morning after we've had some rest."

CHAPTER SEVEN

STEPHANIE

STEPHANIE WOKE TO A furnace burning at her back and a heavy arm across her middle. She lay curled on her side, Triton pressed against her. Some parts of him pressed more insistently than others.

The fire in the stove had gone out, leaving the hut dark. Rain pounded on the roof and ran down the edges of the hut, reminding her of her full bladder. She tried to slip out of bed.

Triton groaned and tightened his arm around her.

"I don't mean to sound indelicate, but if you keep squeezing me, I'm going to burst."

Triton released her with a husky chuckle and rolled to his back. She scurried outside, and set the pail out to fill as she used the prehistoric outhouse again. At least she had walls so she didn't have to do her business where nature could watch her. Her new exhibitionist kink didn't stretch that far.

Stephanie brought fresh water in and they slaked their thirst. She started a fire in the stove and made an early breakfast of cocoa and soup.

After they ate, she checked Triton's injuries. The punctures were clean. And his bruised back was more green than black.

She lay down and faced him.

"How are we going to get off the island? The kayak is too damaged to go anywhere, and there's no way to radio or phone anyone."

Triton, the picture of pain and misery, lay back and draped an arm over his eyes. "My boat will come for us as soon as the seas calm. Maybe later today. Tomorrow at the latest."

"Oh. No wonder you don't seem worried."

"Sorry. Should have mentioned it." He yawned.

She couldn't really blame him for not saying anything. She hadn't asked, and he'd been injured so badly.

"You slept all night. How are you feeling? You feel like you have a fever." She snapped her mouth shut to stop the babbling.

"I run hot, and I feel better." But he still sounded exhausted. "It's not even dawn yet, and far too early to worry about what to do today. Come back to bed."

He was hot and naked under that bedding. "How tired are you?"

"Not *that* tired." He flashed her a naughty smile.

"I've heard sex can be therapeutic."

"I'm willing to give it a shot."

What a way to die if it doesn't work.

Shut up, voice.

Stephanie pulled the blanket down until it exposed his magnificent body to his hips. His arms were as thick around as her thighs. She was no delicate flower, but he made her feel tiny, yet cherished for who and what she was at the same time.

She traced lines over his chest and abs with her fingers before she followed them with her lips and tongue. He hissed in a breath as he watched every one of her movements. His ocean scent filled her nostrils, fueling her desire as her senses were bombarded with the salty taste and exquisite feel of him.

She resisted the impulse to jump into his arms and ease the clamoring need of her body. He would take her, even as injured as he was, but she couldn't stop tasting him and feeling him. She wanted to go slow and savor these moments. Enjoy the power she could have over him now.

"Since you're hurt, you just lay back and let me do all the work. Deal?"

He didn't look like he could put up much of a fight. "Deal. For now." She'd take it.

His skin rippled beneath her mouth as she made her way from his collar bone over his chest to his nipple. She sucked it into her mouth, nibbling with her teeth as she dipped her hand beneath the sheet to cup him.

His shaft jerked, swelling within her grasp when she closed her hand around it and squeezed. The heat of him seared her palm as she slid her thumb over the head, spreading the wet liquid forming there. He was so hard within her hand, yet his skin was so supple. Such a contradiction, much like the loving and tender man before her compared to the often unyielding lover she knew he could be.

The muscles in his forearms stood out as his fingers dug into his palms, but he didn't touch her as she continued her exploration of his body. She grasped the edge of the sheets and pushed them down his thighs, growling when they tangled around his legs.

"You could tear them off me," he suggested helpfully, his voice gruff.

"Like you ruin so many of my clothes?" She laughed as she maneuvered the bedding over his calves and off his feet, so she could toss it aside. "Unlike you, I can restrain myself enough to keep things in one piece, especially since we don't have anymore bedding."

"I've seen you unrestrained."

Her pulse spiked, as did the glint in his eyes when they raked over her and he winked. "If I can't touch you, at least let me see you."

Perhaps it was the power over him having an effect on her, but she believed it was more the look in his eyes emboldening her to slide her hand sensually down the front of her shirt while she rose before him. His eyes followed her hands as she clasped hold of the bottom of her shirt, slid it over her head, and tossed it aside.

"More," he grated.

Stephanie unclasped her bikini bra and lowered first one strap then the other. The turquoise of his eyes darkened, and her body clenched with need. She slipped her bikini top lower, revealing the upper swell of her breasts. His eyes remained latched onto her as he waited for her to take her bra off. She did, inch by inch, until her breasts were bared.

His nostrils flared as his heavy erection jumped. Warm air brushed over her nipples and the need in his gaze caused them to pucker. He licked his lips while he watched them harden. Another rush of power filled her as she realized she held him enthralled without even touching him. She ran her hand down her chest to cup her breast. This felt like another form of someone watching through a window, only now she could see her watcher.

He reached for her, caught himself and stopped. A groan escaped him when she brushed her thumb over her nipple before rolling it between her thumb and index finger. Sliding her hand away from her breast, she ran it over her belly, down to the button on her shorts. She slipped the button free, pushed them down, and kicked them aside. She stood before him in only simple white bikini bottoms.

"The rest," he commanded.

She lifted an eyebrow when his gaze came back to her. Those eyes were a predator's, and he had marked her as his prey.

"Stephanie..." His roughened voice broke off when her hands fell to the waistband of her bikini bottom, and she slid it gradually down her legs before kicking it aside. His eyes latched onto her center, blazing brighter. The wetness between her thighs increased.

"No," she whispered when he moved toward her. "You're hurt." He froze, and his jaw clenched in frustration. With a sway of her hips, she lay aganst him. She sighed when her breasts came into contact with his chest. His erection rubbed against her belly, sending tingles of anticipation through her. Her hands ran over him again as she bent her head to swirl her tongue over his chest.

"You're killing me, Stephanie."

Slowly, she moved over his body, kissing and licking. His head turned so that he could raptly watch her every movement. Her hands slid across shoulders, over the line running down the center of his chest, marveling at the sheer strength and size of him.

He shuddered as she explored him with her hands and mouth, muscles vibrating with restraint. Clasping hold of his hips, she straddled his thighs. Stephanie wrapped her hand around his swollen thickness and slid her hand down to the base of his shaft. She kept her eyes on his as she ran her tongue over the head of his shaft, swallowing the bead of liquid forming on the tip.

She slid her tongue over him before taking his head into her mouth and sucking on it.

"Fuck," he grated. "Take more, Stephanie."

Stephanie barely recognized his voice, it was so gruff, but she obeyed his command. She slid her mouth farther down, swirling her tongue over his skin as she moved. His hips bucked, and the corded muscles in his neck stood out. Her hands slid up his thighs, and she grasped hold of his taut ass with one hand while she used the other to stroke him.

Sweat beaded across his chest and slid down his skin in tantalizing rivulets. He thickened and swelled as she moved faster up and down his length, working him with her mouth and hand.

Watching him, tasting him, was a rush. He still hadn't touched her, yet she was aching for him to be buried deep within her, but no way was she stopping now.

CHAPTER EIGHT

TRITON

"CAN'T TAKE ANYMORE," he ground out as he pulled her up and flipped their positions.

He held her eyes as he placed a kiss against her inner knee before sliding his mouth further up her thigh. Her breath sucked in when his fangs grazed her flesh before he sank them into her. Her body jerked and bowed toward him. Passion darkened her eyes as she watched him.

Sliding his hands beneath her knees, he lifted them over his shoulders until her thighs were on either side of his head. Releasing his bite, he continued to kiss his way up her thigh until his mouth fell upon her hot center. He slipped his hands under her ass to lift her against him.

"Triton!" She panted when he dipped his tongue inside her. She tasted like she smelled — of something sweet like honey. Her fingers entangled in his hair, drawing him closer as her head fell back and she rode his tongue.

He couldn't get enough of savoring her and took in more until he was on the point of coming. When he drew back, he ran his tongue over her clit while sliding one of his fingers into her. He drank in the sight of her body bared before him and his finger deep within her as he pushed her closer to release. Bending back to her, he tongued her clit and spread her further to slip two fingers inside her.

Triton captured her clit between his lips and sucked on it, his tongue circling and grinding against the tiny bundle of nerves. He sucked one of her lower lips into his mouth, skimming his fangs against it, and repeating the same thing on the other side.

Curling his fingers inside her, he stroked her until she jumped when the pad of his thumb hit a spot that made her feel even more turned on.

He rubbed the spot, and his tongue moved back to her clit. He hummed against her, sending vibrations throughout her pussy. Her hands fisted in his hair, her nails scratching his scalp.

"Come, Stephanie. Come for me."

She clutched the sheets as the first wave of an orgasm crashed over her. The muscles of her tight channel gripped his fingers.

One hand went back to his hair, holding her down to him, even as she writhed and wiggled, trying to escape. He gripped her thighs tight. His tongue was restless and drew another orgasm from her.

"Triton... I need..." she began, her breath coming in shallow pants. "A break... too much."

He eased off her clit and g-spot, only stroking her leisurely. Her legs spasmed as she tried to get ahold of herself.

He grinned up at her, and when she was ready, he dove back between her legs and wrung another orgasm from her.

Stephanie tugged on his hair and cried out as she came in a heated rush. The muscles of her sheath rippled around his fingers before he slid them out of her. Her dazed eyes met his.

"Fuck." He shuddered as a bead of cum formed on the head of his cock.

"Triton." Her voice held a warning and she pushed on his shoulders. He let her reverse their positions, and looked up at her, mouth covered in the silky sheen of her arousal. He licked his lips, and kissed her.

Her breasts pressed against his chest, and she guided him to the heat of her entrance. She slid the head of his cock between her folds and partially inside her. Her sheath enveloped him, and the further he pushed into her, the more something changed in him. Stephanie felt right in a way no one ever had before.

Stephanie thrust her hips forward and sank onto him. Her fingers dug into his shoulders as she slid further down the length of him. A shout of possession erupted from him as she cried out and froze when she'd taken all of him. She bit her lower lip, and trembled against him.

"Stephanie?" he asked in a guttural voice.

"I'm fine!"

Triton gripped her nape as he drew her down to inhale her sweet scent and savor the sensation of her exquisite body flush against his. Her thighs banded his hips. Bending her head, she kissed his neck, running her tongue over his skin. His dick jumped inside her as a shiver raced down his spine.

"I feel you deep inside me," she whispered. "I feel every part of you."

He knew what she meant. He felt every movement of the muscles enveloping his shaft, but her emotions came to him, too. Her telepathy was kicking in. She lifted herself until only his head remained inside her before she slid back down the length of him.

"Oh, yes," she moaned.

He guided her movements, gripping her ass with one hand and claiming her mouth. His tongue entangled with hers while her body rose and fell against him. Breaking the kiss, her head fell back, and her wild hair spilled over his fingers as she ground against him and her breasts bobbed with her movements.

He raised his head to run his tongue over her nipple. When he sucked it into his mouth, he nipped at her breast and his fangs pierced her flesh.

Stephanie went wild in his arms. Grinding, thrusting, scratching, she fucked him until he couldn't stand anymore and rose to his knees with her still impaled on him. He bit harder as he laved her nipple.

His movements became more frenzied, and he took her with an abandon bordering on savagery. He tried to reel himself in so as not to hurt her, but her demanding body wouldn't allow him to hold anything back. The pressure building in his dick was becoming unbearable.

Triton pulled his fangs from her breast and sank them into her neck. Her pussy clamped down on his cock in rhythmic spasms as she called his name. Letting go of his tenuous control, he emptied himself into her.

She relaxed against him with contented murmurs as he tucked her into his side and surrendered to healing sleep once more.

CHAPTER NINE

STEPHANIE

SUNLIGHT STREAMED THROUGH the doorway when Stephanie woke the next time. The storm was over. They might be able to leave!

She put a hand on Triton's arm, then yanked it away. Tattoos and hints of scales glowed green on his skin.

What the hell?

Tattoos were one thing, except Triton hadn't had any before... but scales?

Scales!

Stephanie gasped and scooted away so fast she fell out of the bed. The scream welling in her throat came out as a grunt when she landed on her ass.

"Stephanie?" Triton's voice was husky with sleep.

"What's... what's wrong with you?" Her back smacked into a wall. This hut was too tiny to go far. How could he not have told her about this!

"What do you —" Triton sighed. "Oh, fuck. This isn't how I wanted you to find out. The markings aren't contagious. They've appeared because I'm healing."

Don't be scared.

Shut up, *stupid voice! This is definitely a be scared situation!*

"Who...What are you?"

He sat up, rubbed a hand through his hair, and reached for her. "I'm Merrow."

Hurt maintained her distance even as curiosity tried to draw her back toward him. "And what does that mean, exactly?"

"It means... I'm able to change forms."

"Change forms," she repeated stupidly. "Into what?"

"Humans sometimes call us merfolk, or in my case, a merman."

"A... merman." Fish scales, not snake scales. Were fish scales better? She should have been told about the possibility of *any* sort of scales! "You have scales. And a tail."

Now she had to screen her lovers for STDs *and* species? Were there other Merrow or different species at Oubliette? That was amazing! What other kinds were there? Werewolves? Vampires? Ghosts? Bogeymen?

Not only had Triton kept his secret, he'd purposefully locked her out of a whole other world. Did he think so little of her? Maybe she was just a diversion. A human to amuse himself with.

"Sometimes I have a tail, yes." He offered her a grin. "You're welcome to chase it anytime."

She shot to her feet and planted her hands on her hips. "This isn't funny! Were you ever going to tell me? Didn't you think I deserved to know what kind of person I was having sex with?"

The kind of person she'd been having sex with was someone who listened to all her secrets and shared none of his — and Triton had some huge secrets!

Had he been laughing at her the whole time? The human who didn't know anything? Why else would he not tell her? Wasn't there trust between them? She'd loved that feeling as much as the sex. She'd felt she could give herself over to him, and trusted him with every part of her, but apparently she wasn't worthy of the same respect.

Stephanie never thought heartbreak could be a physical sensation, but she swore she felt and heard the snap in her chest.

"Of course you deserve to know, and I swear I was going to explain everything. You're my mate. I don't want to keep secrets from you."

Never from you.

Shut up, *stupid voice*!

"You've got a funny way of showing that. Wait. Your *mate*? What the fuck does *that* mean?" She knew what she thought it meant. At first, her broken heart fluttered excitedly, but she squashed that feeling. That she was supposedly someone important to him, and he'd still kept things from her, only made it worse!

"It means you are meant for me, and I am meant for you."

"Your bites." Stephanie ran a hand over the smooth flesh of her neck. She hadn't missed how bitey he'd been lately, and the way her body reacted. "You do something to me when you bite me, don't you?"

"Yes."

What if birth control didn't work? What if Triton could have been infected her with something? She stiffened. Her new love of ocean. If he was a merman, was that because of him? And the voice, could that be his doing, too?

"You're changing me. You... you... you..." Heartbreak turned to anger. It was one thing to keep his secrets, but when he did something *to her* — Words and thoughts dissolved as rage descended over her in a white hot sheet. "The voice? And wanting to go to the ocean? That's because of you?"

"Yes. Merrow use telepathy to communicate underwater. If I don't bite you again, the effects will wear off. I won't do it again until I've explained everything." Triton took her hands in his. "Stephanie, I'm the same man you've known."

"Except you're *not*," she hissed. "You're something and someone else entirely! And you just decided to change my body to suit you! Does Tessa know what you are?"

She needed him to say no. To tell her that her best friend hadn't been in on the betrayal.

"Maybe. I never told her, but she might have figured it out."

"Why? Is Maclyr a Merrow, too?"

"No. He's not Merrow."

So he might be something else? Stephanie tried to keep her temper and be logical about this. Maclyr wasn't the one trying to put his dick in her, so him keeping his secret from her was fine. And maybe he'd asked Tessa not to tell what he was. That was loyalty, and understandable.

Triton had no excuse.

Stephanie marched for the door. She needed space and there wasn't any in here. There might not be enough space on the whole island. But risking nature's hatred for her was better than standing here like an idiot.

I'm sorry. These words were accompanied a sense of melancholy that nearly stopped her in her tracks.

Shut up, stupid voice.

She followed the trail away from the hut to the dead kayak and plopped down in the sand. Was she overreacting? Maybe. But she was entitled to a bit of overreacting. Betrayal was hard to forgive.

It was only a few minutes later when Triton crouched next to her. "The storm is over. My yacht is here. They'll take you home."

Stephanie scanned the horizon. "How do you know?" The answer came to her. "Telepathy. They're Merrow, too."

Triton pushed to his feet and gestured toward the waves. "They're on the other side of the island and will be here in a few minutes."

The yacht sailed into view, with the addition of some scorch marks, and remained at a distance, as a smaller boat made its way to shore. Finn raised the motor at the back and let the waves carry the boat to the beach, where Triton waded into the water and held it in place.

Knowing what she did now, she studied the other man, trying to find any hints he wasn't human.

"The yacht looks good," Triton said casually. "Everyone all right?"

Stephanie gave Triton a sideways glance. The yacht looked like someone had tried to set it on fire in several places.

"Yes. Nice to see you two weathered the storm." Finn moved to the front of the boat and shook his head at Triton's injuries. "And yes, everyone is fine. We dropped Tessa and Mac off before we came looking for you."

"Thanks for the pick-up."

"No problem. This island was one of the first places we looked." Finn gestured for Stephanie to join him.

She rose, waded into the shallow water, and climbed into the small boat.

Triton waded deeper into the sea and gave their boat a shove.

"Not coming with us, Tri?"

He shook his head. "I'll swim."

She'd pushed him away, but now she felt abandoned. As the launch headed for the yacht, she felt like leaving Triton was the biggest mistake of her life.

Stephanie stood and lifted her hand, but Triton had already dived into the sea. With a flick of his green tail, he disappeared from sight.

He had said she could chase his tail when she liked.

She turned to Finn. "Triton was badly hurt. He probably needs to do more of that glowing green thing before he swims so far."

"You know about us. Sheol owes me twenty bucks. I knew Triton was going to spill the beans."

So he hadn't lied about intending to talk to her.

"Don't worry about Triton. He takes off on his own sometimes, but he always comes back."

Finn helped her aboard the yacht when they arrived. "It really is good to see everyone made it through the fighting. We were worried when those explosions went off and collapsed part of the seacave."

Explosions? "I thought we were in a cave-in."

The Merrow nodded. "Caused by hunters trying to kill us. You didn't think a cave-in shot Triton, did you?"

Shot him? It had been a bullet wound. Not punctures. That huge bruise on Triton's back. And somehow, even with all that, he'd still taken her to the other island somehow, and cared for her while she was unconscious.

Triton had saved her life.

CHAPTER TEN

TRITON

IN HIS FULL MERROW form, Triton drifted in the current a hundred feet below the surface, gills breathing for him as he healed. It had taken all day and most of the evening, but his injuries were gone.

He rose from the depths and swam toward the city. Fully healed, he could swim fast as his yacht sailed, and he arrived in a couple of hours. At nearly four in the morning, the beach was dark and empty when he stopped at a stash the Merrow kept for wardrobe emergencies. At this rate he'd have to restock them all.

What to do about Stephanie? She'd looked disgusted by him. Their relationship wouldn't be the first time a Merrow and a human were mates, but there were no rules for when to come out with, *By the way, I'm not human.*

It was risky, and not just as a matter of the heart. Humans had a habit of killing what they feared or didn't understand, even when they weren't hunters. The more of them who knew, the bigger the risk.

Triton raised a fist and banged on Maclyr's door until he opened it.

The Selkie stood before him wearing shorts, and a scowl that, on any other day, would have made Triton reconsider what he was doing. Maclyr ran his hands through his bed head hair. "What is so important you have to bang on my door at 4am?"

"I need your help, Mac."

"Right now?" He scratched his bare chest and yawned. "With what?"

"Stephanie."

Mac didn't roll his eyes, but it was close.

Triton pointed a finger in Maclyr's face. "Like you did everything perfectly with Tessa?"

"Touche." The Selkie stepped back and opened the door in invitation. "What did you do? Or not do?"

Ignoring the questions, Triton entered the house, and headed to the kitchen. He opened the fridge and blinked in surprise. It was full of... food. Condiments. Vegetables. Fruit. Milk. Juice. "How the fuck is a man supposed to find a beer with all this junk in here?"

Female laughter brought his head up. Tessa stood in the doorway wearing pajama pants and one of Maclyr's old t-shirts. "I'll have you know that's how a fridge is supposed to look. People use them to keep food cold. Beers are in the door."

Triton lifted two, twisted the top off his, handed the other to Maclyr, and sat at the kitchen table.

Tessa filled a mug with water and put it in the microwave. When it dinged, she mixed in a packet of hot cocoa and sat across from him. "What did you do?"

Triton blew a breath out. "Stephanie found out I'm Merrow."

"Found out." Maclyr spun his bottle between his palms. "As in, you didn't tell her."

"I didn't get a chance. We were caught in those explosions. A hunter shot me, and a falling boulder broke half of my body. I was recovering on the island. Being in my half-Merrow form allows me to heal faster. I fell asleep and the shift happened. I always meant to tell her, and about mates, but there was never a good time. But it probably doesn't matter. She's disgusted with what I am."

Tessa sipped her cocoa. "Stephanie is big on trust. I think it's probably more about you not telling her something important than disgust that you're not fully human. She's shared a lot with you."

"So what can I do? Is she a candy and flowers girl?"

Tessa laughed. "No. Well, candy, maybe. But don't give her flowers. She'll think you're trying to kill her with nature."

"Kill her with nature? Humans are so weird." Triton tipped his beer to his mouth and took a big swallow.

"Show her you trust her somehow." Tessa lifted one shoulder. "Explain what happened."

"She didn't want to listen. I need to get her somewhere alone so she has to let me talk." And if she needed a grand gesture to prove he trusted her, he knew precisely where to take her.

"I'll help you, but you better earn her forgiveness, or she's going to stop talking to me, too. She'll definitely not be in the mood for forgiveness at four in the morning, though. Get some rest and we'll call her in a few hours."

TRITON WATCHED THE video feeds of Oubliette from the security room. He worked shifts here and behind the bar. Until Stephanie had walked in and chosen her mask, he'd not felt an urge to visit the playrooms, the fantasy floor, or the strip clubs, although he monitored all those spaces.

On one screen, Tessa and Stephanie sat in a booth eating dinner. Maclyr, working behind the bar, kept casting heated looks at his mate as Tessa devoured her cheeseburger.

Stephanie picked at her food. His mate's wild curls were desperately trying to escape the sleek hairstyle she'd tried to tame them into. He felt some hope that she didn't look entirely happy.

"Thanks for letting me hang out."

Ash, an Ifrit who balanced his love of burning things down with his job as a firefighter, glanced up. He didn't bother hiding his true appearance here. Orange-gold flames flickered in his dark eyes, and the tips of his long black hair glowed like red embers.

"Happy to help out."

"You should know, some hunters attacked my boat the other day. They followed us from the harbor."

"You think it was retaliation for us destroying Sean's house?" The flames in Ash's eyes glowed brighter. He had burned that place to the ground.

Sean had been the leader of a group of hunters until his demise. "Could have been. Or they might have seen us evacuating the Selkies."

"Are any of them still a threat?"

"No. They're dead. Caught in that storm."

"So weird how that storm came out of nowhere." Ash flashed a smirk. "We're going through all paperwork and hard drives we took from Sean's house, compiling that info, and running it through our connections. Hopefully, that'll give us at least a place to start."

"Sheol and Finn are going to dive on the wreckage of the boat, too."

"Good. Let me know if you find anything."

Triton waited impatiently for Stephanie and Tessa to eat dessert — slices of Black Forest birthday cake he'd asked the kitchen to make. Stephanie's favorite.

When their bill was dropped off at their table, Triton slapped Ash on the back. "Thanks, my friend."

The Ifrit glanced up from watching the cameras. "Good luck."

"I might very well need it."

A kidnapping probably wasn't the best approach, but it had worked for Maclyr and Tessa.

Triton lurked in the underground passage where he and Tessa had agreed to meet. He felt Stephanie's approach long before they arrived, and struck fast, using his larger size and paranormal speed. No point in hiding that from any of them now. In seconds, he had Stephanie's wrists and ankles bound, and her body cradled in his arms.

"You *traitor*," Stephanie hissed at Tessa

"Sorry, not sorry." Tessa waved. "Just be glad you're going in style and not the trunk of a car."

Maclyr groaned. "I'm never going to hear the end of that, am I?"

"Just think of all the chances I give you to make it up to me."

Stephanie growled. "You two are *not* cute."

Tessa draped her arms around Maclyr's neck. "We're adorable."

"So sweet you make me sick," Stephanie spat the words, but there was a softness in her eyes. She was happy for her friend, if not with Tessa's part in this kidnapping.

Tessa laughed. "That just means she loves us. You kids go on now. Don't do anything I wouldn't do."

"*Is* there anything you wouldn't do?" Maclyr teased.

"Only one way to find out." She batted her eyes and led him away.

"Kill me now," Stephanie muttered, leaning her head into Triton's chest.

Triton chuckled. "Your death is not part of the plan."

"I haven't ruled out *your* death as part of the plan."

Her anger and snark were much preferred over fear and disgust. She wasn't trying to escape his touch, and she was talking to him. His hopes edged up a notch.

Triton carried her through the tunnels toward the yacht club, ignoring her threats to his life and vital parts of his anatomy. She liked sex too much to carry her threats out.

He hoped.

He marched down the wooden pier and boarded his ship, setting her down in a leather seat on the bridge and casting off.

"Where are you taking me?" Stephanie's furious eyes would have cut him into bait if she could have.

"It's a surprise."

"I'm not sure you'll survive any more surprises."

He laughed and guided his boat into the open ocean.

"It won't be long. Would you like something to drink?"

Stephanie scowled. "No. I'm not going to fall for your Stockholm Syndrome tricks."

No tricks, mate.

She blinked, then her scowl deepened. Good. The telepathy was still working. That would make things easier.

He anchored, stood, and pulled his shirt over his head.

"Don't even think you're getting lucky right now. The only luck you'd have would be if I didn't cut off what you're so proud of."

Triton winced dramatically. "Not my hair!" He knelt to pull off Stephanie's shoes.

She snorted and kicked out at him. "What do you think you're doing?"

"Saving your shoes so you don't have another reason to kill me." He slipped his shorts off, let her ogle him for a moment, and scooped her into his arms. He offered her a broad grin as he strode for the side of the ship.

"Saving my shoes?" Stephanie squirmed frantically in his hold. "Triton!" He climbed onto the railing. "Put me down! I'm tied up and can't swim! Don't you dare —"

The splash they made cut off her words as he landed in the sea and took his Merrow form. He kept them floating with powerful flicks of his tail. Scales and tattoos glowed green as they spread over his skin.

Stephanie stared at the markings. "The scales I get, but what are the designs? Tattoos?"

Triton shook his head. "Each Merrow is born with them. They spread and change as we grow. They tell our history."

I'll breathe for you. Trust me, Stephanie. Please. I'll keep all the nature away.

Stephanie studied his face. Her lips quirked, and she nodded.

Elated, he released her wrists and ankles. She stared at his markings and scales. Their phosphorescence glowed brighter in the ocean. After an eternal minute, her soft fingers touched his skin, tracing the lines of color.

He took them under.

As the water closed over hear head, Stephanie went stiff in his arms. He held her closer and pressed his lips to hers. She tasted of chocolate, and cherries, and frosting. Black Forest cake quckly rose to the top of his favorite-things-to-eat list.

She'd probably had enough serum to hold her breath for as long as this would take, but he couldn't deny himself the chance to kiss her. To do something so intimate as breathe for her.

Breathe, mate. As often as you need to. It won't take long to get where we're going.

Davy Jones' locker?

He chuckled. *Not quite that deep.*

Stephanie wrapped her legs around his hips and her arms around his neck as she fed at his mouth and he went deeper into the ocean.

The change in pressure as he passed through the thermocline-like boundary always felt like coming home, which it was, in a way.

Stephanie jolted in his arms and pulled her mouth away from his. She stared at their surroundings, wide-eyed.

In a black sea, pure magic glittered like thousands of stars in a clear night sky.

She blinked several times and gasped. "What is this place? How is there air? Why am I dry?" She swished her hand around. "I still feel water."

"We're not in your ocean anymore. Not completely anyway. I thought you'd like this place after you talked about stars when we saw the glowworms. The Merrow call this the Sea of Stars."

"It's beautiful." She stretched an arm out and extended a finger toward the nearest twinkle. The magic didn't allow anyone to touch it, but when Stephanie held out a cupped palm, the sparkle hovered over her skin.

"Stephanie, this is the most closely guarded secret I have. Even more than what I am."

"I can see why. It's amazing. You'd be overrun with people who wanted to see it."

"It is beautiful, but that's not what makes this place special."

"Then what?"

He hoped he was doing the right thing. "It's a portal to our world. There are a few of them. In showing this to you, I'm trusting you with the lives of all the Merrow."

She stared at him. "All the Merrow? Your world?"

"You'd call it another dimension. Other Worlders are called Other Worlders for a reason."

"What's your home called?"

"Merrow just call it home. Humans have given it a few names. Atlantis is one."

"Atlantis! An underwater city? Will you take me there?"

"Yes. We just need to talk about a few more things first."

Stephanie leveled him with a look that dared him to defy her. "Are you going to tell me why you didn't tell me about you being Merrow? You should have told me you were changing my body. We'd known each other for a month at Oubliette. You could have told me at any time."

"No, I couldn't." He met her eyes and pleaded for understanding. "There are spells and wards in place at the club to keep us from divulging anything to do with what we are. I'm not the only Other Worlder there. No pillow talk that might reveal secrets is permitted. I wouldn't be the only one at risk."

"Oh. I guess that makes sense." She traced one of the markings glowing on his skin.

"That left the day of the cave-in when we were both injured and exhausted, which didn't seem the best time for such a discussion. The next day you woke before me and the secret was out. Will you forgive me?"

She tilted her head. "I suppose I could cut you some slack since you saved my life. Finn told me about the explosions and your bullet wound, which you also kept secret from me, but I will graciously include those things under the umbrella of the saving my life. Going forward, you have to promise to tell me everything you know about Other Worlders."

"I promise I will tell you everything from now on, unless the secrets are not mine. Before you get angry, I'm sure there are things about Tessa you won't tell me, or that you don't want her to tell Maclyr about you. I will only keep those kinds of things from you, and won't blame you for doing the same. Deal?"

"Fair enough. Let's start with this, then. If you keep biting me, how will I change? Will I still be human?"

"Human with special abilities. Your telepathy will develop. You'll be able to hold your breath for a long time, and bear my children."

"Children!" She jolted upright in his arms.

He held her tighter. "If we choose to have them, they'll be born Merrow."

"Can we go to Atlantis now?"

Triton let her change the subject. Kids weren't a priority now, and she knew what she needed to. "I have to tell you one more thing."

"You're full of secrets, aren't you?" She laughed. "What is it?"

"I'm the king of that world."

Stephanie laughed.

He didn't. "Some people might treat me differently."

"You're serious?"

"It's a job. Like being a CEO or any other position of power. We're appointed, and not paid. I protect the Merrow, but the riches of the realm don't belong to me. I own my personal fortune and nothing else."

"Is that why you're so mate-minded? For an heir because you're king?"

"I'm mate-minded because you are irresistible to me. Having a mate isn't required for being king." He snorted. "Only humans think because one man or woman made a good ruler that their descendants automatically would or are entitled to power."

"Hey! We don't all think that way."

"I'm just saying genetics doesn't entitle someone to rule. That was never a consideration for me being with you. Being able to have children just gives us the choice."

"Oh." She shifted in his arms. Again she seemed uncomfortable with the idea of kids. He wouldn't push for now.

"Ready to go? We have nature in my home." He pressed his lips to her forehead. "But I won't let any of the bad nature get you."

"Tessa has a big mouth." Stephanie hugged him, pulled back, and gave him a naughty curve of her lips. "Between saving me from nature and the sex, I am starting to think having you around might not be so bad."

"I suppose I can settle for that for now." Triton flicked his tail to get them moving. The stars blurred as he traveled through the portal, pushing through another boundary.

As they exited into a sapphire blue sea, magic rolled over him in swells. A supertide.

A curious octopus regarded them with its big, round eyes. A blue whale and her twin calves filled the water with beautiful songs. Sharks, schools of fish, turtles, cuttlefish, mantas, and jellyfish all congregated in the magically charged ocean.

So. Much. Nature! Stephanie's thought shouted.

They're only here for the magic. I've got you. Listen to the whales. That song is only sung here.

Stephanie closed her eyes and cocked her head, a happy smile on her face as she listened.

Triton swam toward the city nestled in a volcanic crater. He tapped Stephanie on the shoulder and she peered up at him. He tilted his head, and she turned hers, eyes widening.

Atlantis was a sprawling city constructed of coral, stone, and volcanic rock. Towers and spires soared hundreds of feet high, connected by bridges at varying levels. Kelp and brightly colored ocean plants crawled up the architecture.

Merrow and other ingabitants looked out the windows of their homes and waved. Others worked in fields tending fish, kelp, and oyster farms.

Triton swam with Stephanie toward his tower of obsidian, covered by soft corals. He changed to his human form, entered his air bedroom, and set Stephanie on her feet.

"Welcome to my home."

Bioluminescent glows in water lamps lit the space. His bed of a soft coral was draped in woven seagrass and huge fronds of kelp. Uneven protrusions of volcanic rock provided shelf space, and hard coral growing along the walls provided places for hanging clothes.

He didn't keep much in his bedroom. Other spaces kept his treasures and magic safe.

Stephanie took everything in at a glance as she moved around his space. "Why do you need bridges? Can't everyone swim everywhere? Why can I breathe in here? This isn't anything like I thought Atlantis would be."

He loved her enthusiasm. "There are other underwater cities, but humans tend to lump them together. We receive visitors from Other Worlds. The bridges are for anyone who would prefer to walk, and we have double rooms — one with water and one with air. Wards keep the water out."

"You have a bedroom full of water?" She rubbed her arms and paced like she was cold. "That gives a whole new meaning to breath play."

Triton caught her, ran his hands up her ribs and cupped her breasts. "You could breathe from me the entire time."

She arched into his caresses. "I've always liked the way you touch me, but it feels different here. What is that strange feeling? It feels like... I don't know. Some sort of pressure. I feel restless."

"I feel it, too. The portals let magic through. Sometimes the magics from other worlds converge with the rise of magic here and we get a supertide. That's what you're feeling. They're unpredictable. Any magic used while it's flowing will be increased."

"Including whatever makes us mates?"

He pinched her tightening nipples. "Yes. Does that frighten you?" Leaving one breast, he slid a hand down her body to the juncture of her thighs and cupped her.

Stephanie's breath caught. "No." She pulled out of his grasp and faced him. "It's not fear I'm feeling."

Triton gave her a lazy smile. "Strip for me, Stephanie."

"Right here in front of this window?" Her eyes gleamed. "There's an entire city of Merrow out there."

"I guarantee you someone will see."

"And they'll see the king having his way with... what am I? A consort?" She narrowed her eyes at him. "I better be the *only* consort."

"You are, Stephanie." He licked a line down her neck. "We're mates." He nipped her throat. "You are the only woman for me, and you don't need a title dependent on mine to define you. Whoever watches will see the king on his knees pleasuring you." Warm breath carried the last words over her ear, sending a shiver through her.

Stephanie arched a sassy eyebrow. "Well, as long as the king is the one on his knees this time." She pulled her shirt over her head, sending her pants and undergarments to join it on the floor.

He backed her against the window and turned her sideways. "Keep your hands above your head or playing with your nipples. Don't touch me."

Her chin rose. "In case you forgot, you may be king here, but you're not the king of me."

"But it's my tongue that won't be inside you if you don't do as I say."

"Not fair!"

He stopped further debate and argument by covering her mouth with his. She kissed him, wrapping her arms around his neck, and turning aggressor.

Her exploration of his mouth quickened into a bruising possession. He met her demands, then took more, stealing her very breath. She clung to him, digging her nails into his shoulders.

His dick hurt, aching with the need to experience Stephanie's soft core. He'd never been this hard before. Never felt as if he was going to die if he didn't get inside a woman. Now.

Was this a mate thing? A supertide thing? A combination?

Triton broke off to lay kisses across her jawline. He sucked on her neck, right over her pulse, and bit. She let her head fall back, exposing more of the long column of her throat to him. Unable to resist, he moved to the other side of her delicate throat and bit her again.

The magic of the supertide surged in his blood, making the urge to share his serum with his mate overwhelming. As soon as he bit her, more serum built up in him, burning in his blood and fangs.

As he knelt, his gaze latched on to her pert nipples, and he bent his head to suck one into his mouth. Her fingers entwined in his hair as she held him close.

"Bite me," she whispered.

Triton sank his fangs into her breast, and she cried out as she arched into him. He nipped her other breast, tugging on the erect tip, before sinking his fangs into her again.

Kissing and licking his way down her stomach, he slid his hands up her inner thighs to spread her legs and expose her already glistening core. The scent of her arousal teased him. With her thighs held open, he dipped his head and licked her.

He sank his fangs into her thigh, more forcefully than he intended. Stephanie gave a startled shriek that turned into a moan as the bite went on.

I love it when you bite me.

Lucky for you, since I'm going to bite you everywhere.

Power energized him, and took his lust up a notch. He draped her legs over his shoulders, lifted her, and buried his face in her pussy. Her moans spurred him on. He dragged his tongue through her cleft, spreading her lips wide and flicking her hard clit with each pass.

Her flavor was richer on his tongue from all the super-charged serum he'd given her. She was more sensitive too. With a single swipe of his tongue, she groaned.

Her enjoyment pleased him. An animalistic sound rumbled in his chest. Stephanie whimpered. The sound inflamed him. He thrust his tongue into her opening, over and over until her tight channel gripped him.

Stephanie was going to come.

He moved his thumb to her clit and curled his tongue, stroking into her. Her body arched on an orgasm that opened her mouth in a silent cry and fed him her passion.

She twisted her fingers around the collar of his shirt and yanked. "Take me to bed."

Triton carried her to the bed, laid her down, and crawled over her.

"This mattress and bedding feels a lot like nature."

"It's good nature. I promise my bed won't hurt you."

She lifted her head for his kiss. He couldn't deny her for a few seconds. Chest heaving, he turned his head, breaking their kiss. "Are you ready for my cock?"

"Yes." The word matched her pleading tone. He brushed his lips over hers one more time and eased back. Stephanie's fingernails marked a trail down his arms. The small bite of pain appealed to him.

The head of his cock slid through her arousal. His dick jerked. He'd waited too long. He couldn't tease Stephanie any longer. He pressed his palm against her lower belly, holding her in place, and pushed the head of his dick into her opening.

He'd never experienced such exquisite gratification. It bordered on pain as his cock swelled more than it ever had.

The tide was rising, along with its energy in his blood. Where the power came from, he didn't know, but his body understood its effect.

A guttural moan escaped his throat as her core clamped down, fighting his possession. Stephanie's breathy groan matched his. She wanted him. His cock was long, and aching. Rolling his hips, he worked into Stephanie's body. Each forward drive pushed his dick farther into her tight core.

One more rolling thrust joined them. The strangling grip of her body eased. He'd be able to ride her hard. Instead of giving in to the desire, he stilled with his dick partially inside Stephanie's pussy.

"You're tight." He kissed her neck. "But wet, hot, and so soft. I want to stay inside you forever." He caressed her belly before sliding his fingers lower to where her lower lips stretched around his shaft.

His balls drew up as pure need blindsided him. He could come easily, without having to ride Stephanie at all.

A rough curse escaped his throat. He willed his damn dick into submission. He planned on coming multiple times tonight. His cock could be patient.

During the supertide, magic would flow over them, amplifying a compulsion neither of them would ever be able to ignore. They'd crave the passion they could create together. The pressure in his balls eased. Moving his hand out of the way, he bit the inside of his mouth and drove his hard length deep.

His groin smacked Stephanie's body, sliding her body up the bed. He repeated the hard drive, again and again. Stephanie's body, impaled on his full length each time, tightened and squeezed him, making the ache in his shaft grow.

He thrust faster, harder. Stephanie's body accepted his, welcoming his rough thrusts with a wash of arousal that slickened his dick. He slid his hand over her inner leg, then to her clit. A quick flick to the nub sent small waves rippling over his shaft.

Careful not to put his full weight on her, he rode her body. The race to completion overcame him. Breathing hard, he took his pleasure from her. His dick thickened, and his balls drew up. He was going to come.

The tight grip of Stephanie's core meant she was, too. The moment he stopped moving, she'd fall over the edge.

"Feels good." Stephanie whimpered. "You feel so good inside me."

He gripped her hip as he held her in place, drumming into her, her pussy clenching around him and milking his cock. He stroked her swollen nub, gritting his teeth and hanging onto his restraint until she moaned.

Her sex clamped down, and he finally let go. His release thundered through him. They held still together with him curled over her, their breath heaving.

Rolling, he drew her with him, stroking her back and hair until she dozed off.

He let himself sleep, but woke when Stephanie shifted restlessly. His gaze ran over his mate sprawled on top of him, hand beneath her head on his chest as she slept. He'd bitten her, perhaps too much — visible marks on her neck, shoulders, breasts, and thighs. He'd been rough, but he hadn't been able to stop himself.

"Triton," Stephanie murmured. Her lashes fluttered against his skin and her eyes danced under her closed lids as she changed. He rested his hands on the small of her back, pulling her closer. His touch settled her, as it usually did, and he waited for her to wake.

CHAPTER ELEVEN

STEPHANIE

THIS SUPERTIDE WAS going to be the death of her. Stephanie had lost track of the number of times they lost themselves in one another. She'd had dozens of orgasms. Her body was full of serum from all the bites. But the magical pressure built inside her again, and she needed more.

She should be sated and sore, but her blood thrummed through her and her body tingled in anticipation.

They hadn't left the bed, much less the bedroom. Thankfully, Triton was able to keep up with her demands.

Her breath hitched, and she bit her lip as his finger stilled on her nipple. His breath warmed her chest. She sighed when his tongue swirled over her breast. His fangs scraped her skin, but he didn't bite, even though she wanted him to.

Stephanie rode his thigh, moaning at the blissful friction until he removed his leg from between hers.

She bit back a groan, but he grabbed her waist and rolled her over. A shiver raced over her skin when he ran his finger down her spine before trailing it with his tongue.

"Triton," Stephanie panted when his palm slid between her thighs to massage her and his finger teased her aching center through her pants. She thrust her hips backward when he took his hand away from where she needed it.

She had to see him, to feel him, but he pushed his chest against her back.

"Put your arms over your head." He maneuvered her up the bed until her palms rested against the jagged rocks. One of his powerful hands slid up to cup her breast. His roughened palm ran over her stomach as he rose, sending goose bumps across her skin.

Her legs spread further apart when his fingers pressed between her thighs. His chest burned into her back when he moulded himself around her. His ragged breath sounded in her ear as he ran his tongue leisurely over it and nipped at her earlobe.

Stephanie's hands flattened against the rock when his thick finger dipped into her, and he stroked her leisurely back and forth, spreading her wetness. The hot length of his erection pressed against her lower back as he jerked her more firmly against him.

"Triton!" She gasped when he dipped another finger into her, stretching her. Her entire world focused on the delicious sensations evoked by his touch.

His other hand fondled her breast, thumb and forefinger tweaking her nipple as he rolled it between his fingers. His mouth left a trail of kisses across her shoulder and up to her other ear as he nudged her legs wider.

His shaft slid between her thighs, teasing as it slipped across her wet flesh. "Do you like that?" he inquired as he pulled his hips back and thrust forward again, but he didn't enter her, didn't end the torment. "Answer me, Stephanie."

"Yes!" she cried. "You know I do."

Wrapping a hand in her hair, he turned her head to the side until his lips brushed hers. "Do you want me inside of you?"

Right then, she couldn't think of anything she wanted more as his ocean scent engulfed her and his powerful body enfolded hers. "Yes."

His mouth curved into a smile against her neck. He surged forward again before pulling away from her. "Beg me for it." This time when he thrust forward, his thumb dipped down to rub against her clit. A tsunami of pleasure rocked her. She arched against him when his hand caressed her breasts.

"Stephanie," he growled, and she sensed his unraveling control as he thrust faster between her thighs. She could deny him her begging, and he would still give in to her, still give her what she so desperately craved, but she was helpless to deny him what he asked for.

"Please, Triton," she begged when he stroked her clit again. "I need you inside of me, now."

His hand slid between her legs again, but this time he didn't tease her as he took hold of his swollen shaft and guided it into her. She groaned at the sensation of his thick erection slipping deep within her. He filled her so completely tha he throbbed inside her. He grabbed her waist and withdrew until only his head remained within her, and slid into her again.

She pushed back, demanding more with her body as she bent lower to give him better access. His fingers dug into her skin as he pulled out of her and drove in again. His sweat-slicked body surrounded her as he moved faster and deeper within her.

Her head spun as the pleasure only his body could give swamped her. Releasing her with one hand, he slid it between her thighs to fondle her clit again as he continued to drive fiercely into her.

Her body fractured beneath his expert fingers and pummeling hips. Her legs gave out, but his hold kept her hips high. She felt no trepidation when his hand caged her throat, and he pulled her head back. His tongue swirled over her flesh before he sank his fangs into her shoulder.

Another orgasm rocked her as he drove relentlessly between her thighs while leaving his mark on her. Her muscles clenched around his swollen length, gripping him within her. He threw his head back and bellowed in ecstasy when he found his release.

His head fell into the crook of her neck. Gathering her to him, he rolled onto his back and when she settled into him, he ran his fingers through her wild auburn tangle of hair.

This time, the magical surge that had taken hold of her eased and she slumped in relief. "Is it over?"

"Yes. the tide is in ebb."

"How long has it been?"

"All night. It's morning now."

"I didn't think it would ever end." Stephanie blew out a relieved breath as thoughts of things other than sex filled her mind. "Will you show me more Other Worlds?"

"If you like." His voice rumbled through her. "I'll even protect you from evil nature wherever we go."

Stephanie lifted her head and glared at him. "In case you have any doubts, that is an automatic official prerequisite for whenever we are together and whatever world we're in."

He chuckled. "Seems like you have some new boundaries for me to push."

She smiled and laid her head back down, listening to his heart. "A few days ago, all I cared about was taking my finals. Now hunters have tried to kill me. I survived an entire island of nature. I've discovered Other Worlders, and traveled to a version of Atlantis where I dallied with the king during a magical supertide."

Maybe it was the magic and serum running through her, but right now, she felt like she could handle anything.

"Are there more hunters? Will they try to hurt you again?"

His fingers twined and loosened in her hair. "It seems like there are always people who want to hurt anyone different from themselves. The group coming after me now is big. We don't know how many members they have, and they're well funded. We're going through some files we got our hands on. It won't be a short fight."

She shifted in his hold to face him. "Who is we? More Merrow?"

"Some. There are aso a Barghest, an Ifrit, an Incubus, and some shifters."

"Would they have a problem working with me?"

He studied her face. "Are you secretly a ninja?"

"Not *that* way." She thumped his chest. "I double majored in computer science and finance. You said the hunters are well funded? What would happen if we tracked all their money and took it away?"

"Stephanie." Triton sat up and cradled her face in his palms. "They may very well have more than one source, but one of them is Tessa's father. I don't want to cause issues between you and your friend."

"I have *never* liked that bastard." She'd had to watch helplessly as that man controlled and smothered Tessa for years. So many times, she'd offered to help Tessa escape, and her friend had always refused, fearing what her father would do to Stephanie and her family.

"Tessa has no love for him, either. I know my friend, and she would tell us to do what we have to. If we get to destroy that man's life in the process of saving yours, count me in."

A slow smile curved Triton's lips and his turquoise eyes darkened. "My mate is sexy when she gets vengeful."

She snorted. "You would think I'm sexy no matter what."

"True." He kissed her — a long, lazy kiss that made her tingle anew. "When we go back, I'll introduce you to the others. We'll show you everything we have on the hunters."

"Good." Stephanie laid her head on Triton's chest. "I'll make them wish it was only nature coming for them."

THANK YOU

Thank you for sticking with the story to the end! If you enjoyed it, please consider leaving a review. A couple of words, or even just a rating from you can help others find my work, which will encourage me to write more stories!

ABOUT THE AUTHOR

I love to travel, read, and think of ways to complicate my characters' lives. I have two borrowed cats who take shameless advantage of my good nature. Hopefully you find my characters a lot more entertaining than I am. :)

If you enjoyed this story, you may be interested to know that I write in several series. While each novel is written for one relationship, features unique mythologies, and can be read as standalone, a little more of that world is revealed and the overall arc of the series grows throughout.

The best way to find out what's going on with the series, and me, is to visit my website at https://www.ysobellablack.com. There, you can check out the wikis and timelines for each series. Or, sign up for the newsletter.

https://ysobellablack.com/newsletter/

I send out things like surveys, freebies, contests, and random news about things going on with me that may or may not be interesting.

I love hearing from my readers. Feel free to send me an email at ysobella@ysobellablack.com.

Or find me here:

Twitter[1]

Pinterest[2]

Goodreads[3]

Instagram[4]

---

1. https://twitter.com/ysobellablack

2. https://pinterest.com/ysobellablack/

3. https://www.goodreads.com/ysobellablack

4. https://www.instagram.com/ysobellablackauthor/

<u>TikTok</u>[5]
<u>Bookbub</u>[6]

---

5. http://www.tiktok.com/ysobellablack

6. http://www.bookbub.com/ysobellablack

Written as Ysobel Black (Nice/Sweet Versions)

Bakery Street Cozy Mysteries

Paranormal Cozy Mysteries
The Lyrical Lycanthrope

Fairy Tales With a Twist

Retellings of fairy tales, myths, and stories you only thought you knew.
The Crimson Hood & the Alpha of Wolves
The Ice Maiden & the Princes of Diamonds

Holiday Hullabaloo

Love in Ashana can be tricky, but twelve days of chaos result in
paranormal happily-ever-afters.
A Penghou in a Pine Tree
Two Tatzelwurms
Three French Bêtes
Four Ceffyl Dŵr
Five Golden Wings
Six Grootslangs Playing

Seven Spawns a-Swimming
Eight Maenads Mixing
Nine Lazy Dragons
Ten Swords a-Sneaking
Eleven Pixie Potions
Twelve Lovers Loving

Pohjola Maidens

The Maidens of Pohjola are free, heading for the human world, and looking for love.
Dream's Sleeper: Lemminki

Strygoi Witches & Vampires

Join an Ildum of vampires over 10,000 years of history and mythology as they find their Dragăs — witches who make their hearts beat and restore their souls..
Ember's Light: Stryx
Viktoria's Shadow: Jael
Myth's Legend: Norrix
Bijou's Cure: Zeke
Musette's Fate: Idris

Strygoi Witches & Vampires Companion Stories

Shadowy — Viktoria's prequel (companion novella)
Echo's Answer: Lachlan (companion novel)

COLLECTIONS/BOX SETS

Holiday Hullabaloo
DAYS 1-12

Strygoi Witches & Vampires
COLLECTION ONE: BOOKS 1-4

Written as Ysobella Black (Naughty/Steamy Versions)

Alix in Wonderland

A reverse harem (MFMMM) retelling of Alice in Wonderland.
Madness of the Hatter

Bakery Street Mysteries

Paranormal Cozy-ish Mysteries
The Lyrical Lycanthrope

Fairy Tales With a Kink

Retellings of fairy tales, myths, and stories you only thought you knew.
The Crimson Hood & the Alpha of Wolves
The Ice Maiden & the Princes of Diamonds

Grove of Bandrui

Immortal Druids search for their Maités.
Druid of Oaks
Druid of Apples

Harom & Aneja

Witches choose three men to form their Haroms as they become Aneja
— Walkers in magic. Reverse Harem (MFMM)
RealmWalker
BeastWalker

Magical Love in London

Regency London with a paranormal twist.
Marriage of Inconvenience

Oubliette

Paranormal short and steamy stories.
Selkie
Merrow

Pohjola Passions

The Maidens of Pohjola are free, on their way to the human world, and
looking for love.
Dream's Sleeper: Lemminki

Raven Chronicles: Phoenix Rising

The battle for the Raven Throne in the Inisfail Fae Court is full of war,
sex, and intrigue that spans generations.

First Generation

Souls Lost & Found

Once in a blue moon, star-crossed lovers get a second chance for their love to shine.
The Egyptian

Utopia Pack

A pack of shifters find their Fateds.
Unyielding

Vampires & Strygoi Witches

Join an Ildum of vampires over 10,000 years of history and mythology as they find their Dragăs — witches who make their hearts beat and restore their souls.
Ember's Light: Stryx
Viktoria's Shadow: Jael
Myth's Legend: Norrix
Bijou's Cure: Zeke
Musette's Fate: Idris

Vampires & Strygoi Witches Companion Stories

Shadowy — Viktoria's Prequel
Echo's Answer: Lachlan

Xov & Xau

In a war where each side is determined to inherit the earth, sparks fly.
And when Xov finds Xau, a different sort of sparks ignite.
Poisoned Heart

Yuletide Chaos

Love in Ashana can be tricky, but twelve days of chaos result in
paranormal happily-ever-afters.
A Penghou in a Pine Tree
Two Tatzelwurms
Three French Bêtes
Four Ceffyl Dŵr
Five Golden Wings
Six Grootslangs Playing
Seven Spawns a-Swimming
Eight Maenads Mixing
Nine Lazy Dragons
Ten Swords a-Sneaking
Eleven Pixie Potions
Twelve Lovers Loving

COLLECTIONS/BOX SETS

Three First in a Series

FATED – Three Firsts

Ember's Light:Stryx
RealmWalker
Poisoned Heart

Five First in a Series

FATED – Five Firsts
Ember's Light:Stryx
The Crimson Hood & the Alpha of Wolves
RealmWalker
Dream's Sleeper: Lemminki
Poisoned Heart

Vampires & Strygoi Witches

COLLECTION ONE: BOOKS 1-4

Yuletide Yearnings

Yuletide Chaos, Days 1-12